EGMONT

We bring stories to life

This edition published in Great Britain 2010 by Dean,
an imprint of Egmont UK Limited
239 Kensington High Street, London W8 6SA
All Rights Reserved

HiT entertainment

ISBN 978 0 6035 6524 3
1 3 5 7 9 10 8 6 4 2
Printed and bound in Italy

Thomas in Trouble

It was a busy day for the engines
on The Fat Controller's railway.

Gordon was taking passengers
across the Island. He felt splendid.

Henry was delivering logs to the
Timber Yards. He was right on time!

Percy was pleased to be pulling Mail Trucks and James was happily hauling flatbeds.

But Thomas and Emily were at the Fitter's Yard for repairs.

"I can't wait to get back to work," peeped Thomas. "I am taking the School Choir to their concert!"

Soon, Emily was ready to go back to work but Thomas had to stay behind and wait for his final inspection.

"Goodbye, Thomas," Emily whistled. "Good luck."

Thomas was still waiting for his inspection when James puffed in to the Yard to deliver some paint.

"Bust my boiler!" James laughed. "You have broken down, Thomas!"

"No, I haven't!" huffed Thomas, crossly.

"You must have done," snorted
James. "Otherwise you wouldn't be
at the Fitter's Yard. What a shame
you're not a smart and Useful
Engine like me!"

Just then, The Fat Controller arrived. "Thomas!" he boomed. "Are you ready to take the School Choir to their concert?"

"Nearly ready, Sir," puffed Thomas, excitedly.

"Nearly ready is not good enough!"
The Fat Controller replied.

Thomas didn't want anyone else to
collect the Choir — carrying the
children was his favourite job.
He decided he would leave before
his final inspection.

"I'm ready now, Sir!" he puffed.
The Fat Controller was pleased.
Thomas quickly puffed out of
the Fitter's Yard to pick up his
carriages, Annie and Clarabel.

Further down the line, Thomas
began to make some very strange
noises.

"Clangety-clong, something's wrong!" sang Annie and Clarabel. They could tell something was wrong with Thomas.
But Thomas wasn't listening. He was too excited about collecting the School Choir.

The School Choir
cheered
as soon as
they saw
Thomas.

"All aboard!"
chuffed Thomas
as he 'clangety-clonged' into
Knapford Station.

"Who is making that nasty noise?" wheeshed Emily. "Did you have your final inspection, Thomas?"

This made Thomas cross. "I'm fine!" Thomas huffed.

The Choir got on board and he steamed away. Thomas rattled even more, "Clangety-clong, clangety-clong!"

Thomas had to stop at a signal; he was feeling very hot and bothered.

Toby saw that something was wrong. "Did you take on enough water at the Fitter's Yard?" he asked, kindly.

"There's nothing wrong with me!"
replied Thomas, crossly.

Just then the signal changed and
Thomas puffed away, noisily.

When Percy saw Thomas at a level crossing further up the line, he was rattling and steaming more and more.

"What's happened to you?" peeped Percy. "You looked all puffed out!"

Thomas didn't like being told there was something wrong with him, so when the barrier opened he huffed away.
"Clangety-clong, clangety-clong."

Then there was trouble! Thomas began to chuff slower and slower and slower.

"I need a rest!" Thomas gasped, as he 'clangety-clonged' into a siding.

Steam burst from his boiler and black smoke flew from his funnel. With a final rattle, Thomas broke down! He felt terrible.

The School Choir began to sing
while they waited.

"The children will be late for
their concert and it's all my fault,"
Thomas wailed, sadly. "I've let
everyone down." He was upset.

Just then, Gordon puffed around
the bend.

Gordon could see that Thomas
was in trouble but he couldn't stop
to help because he had his own
passengers on board.

"Sorry, Thomas," steamed Gordon.
"I'm a guaranteed connection."

"Now what am I going to do?" cried
Thomas. He was very worried.

Just then, Thomas heard a whistle.
It was James! Thomas tooted as
loudly as he could. "Stop!"

"Bust my boiler!" laughed James.
"I said you were a broken down
little engine!"

"I am," sighed Thomas. "And I
need your help. Can you take the
children to their concert?"

James didn't laugh at Thomas.
He could see that Thomas was in
trouble, and he was happy to help
his friend. "I'll get them there on
time!" he promised.

Thomas knew he had to get back to the Yard to be repaired as soon as possible.

Henry was sent to collect Thomas.

He soon arrived and quickly shunted Thomas to the Fitter's Yard.

Before long, Thomas was as good as new! And this time he waited patiently for his final inspection!

"You have been very patient, Thomas," said The Fat Controller. "As a reward, I have a special job for you."

Thomas was delighted; he wondered what the special job could be.

"Thomas," he announced. "Now you are fixed, you are to collect the School Choir and bring them home again."

"Oh, thank you, Sir!" tooted Thomas, happily.

Thomas chuffed to the concert, "Clangety-clong, nothing is wrong!" he laughed.